We're Very Good Friends, My Grandpa and I

Written and Illustrated by

P.K. Hallinan

For Fla, with love.

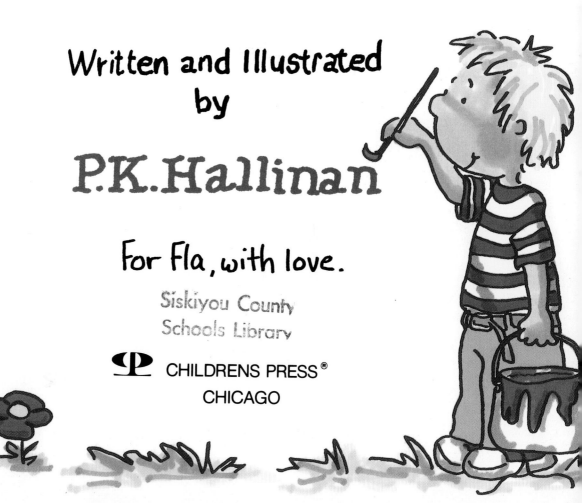

CP CHILDRENS PRESS ®

CHICAGO

Library of Congress Cataloging-in-Publication Data

Hallinan, P. K.
  We're very good friends, my grandpa and I / written and
illustrated by P.K. Hallinan.
      p.   cm.
  Summary: Relates, in verse, why it's fun to spend the day with
Grandpa.
  ISBN 0-516-03653-X
  [1. Grandfathers—Fiction. 2. Stories in rhyme.] I. Title.
PZ8.3.H15Wh   1989
[E]—dc19   88-26881
                                                         CIP
                                                          AC

We're very good friends,
my grandpa and I.

We like to take walks...

And watch cars drive by.

And sometimes he goes
just a little bit slow,
but that's fine with me—
we're good friends, you know.

We do lots of neat things,
my grandpa and I.

We cook up French toast;

we go hunting for ghosts.

We laugh with our eyes
about Grandma's burnt roasts.

And sometimes we just sit
and we don't talk at all.
But that's okay, too;
we're friends, after all.

We always have fun,
my grandpa and I.

We whistle to birds
and offer them bread.

We walk to the beach
with our hats on our heads.

We even go shopping
and dance down the aisles
with Grandpa's soft-shoe
bringing all kinds of smiles.   17

And frankly we're happy
to spend the whole day
just being together
in wonderful ways...

or painting some flowers
on old coffee cups,

or maybe just sorting through
Grandpa's old files
and putting the papers
in six different piles.

We make quite a team,
my grandpa and I.

Then in the evening
it's time for a story—
how Grandpa saved Europe
while waving Old Glory!

But if he starts yawning
and takes a short nap,
I just like to stay there
curled up on his lap.

And I know deep inside
he always will be
a part of my heart
with his words guiding me.

For Grandpa is special
in ways that don't end...

And he knows every secret
of being a friend.

So when all's said and done,
I guess LOVE is why...

we're very good friends,
my grandpa and I.

ABOUT P. K. HALLINAN

Patrick Hallinan began writing children's books at the request of his wife who asked him to create an original Christmas gift for their two young sons. Today, nearly twenty years later, P. K. Hallinan is one of America's foremost authors of children's books that teach personal values and self-awareness. His sensitive text and heartwarming illustrations offer a celebration of life to all who visit his very special world.

The little character who appears throughout Mr. Hallinan's books is "P. K.", a blend of his two real-life sons, Kenneth and Michael. Although "P. K." has taken on his own personality over the years, Mr. Hallinan feels that he represents "all children, young and old, who see the world through the eyes of innocence."

Mr. Hallinan lives with his wife, Jeanne, and their three dogs in southern California.